Read all the
Gargoylz adventures!

Gargoylz on the Loose!

Gargoylz Get Up to Mischief

Gargoylz at a Midnight Feast

Gargoylz Take a Trip

Gargoylz Put On a Show

Gargoylz Have Fun at the Fair

Gargoylz

Have Fun at the Fair

Burchett & Vogler

illustrated by Leighton Noyes

RED FOX

GARGOYLZ HAVE FUN AT THE FAIR
A RED FOX BOOK 978 1 849 41034 2
First published in Great Britain by Red Fox,
an imprint of Random House Children's Books
A Random House Group Company

This edition published 2010

1 3 5 7 9 10 8 6 4 2

Series created and developed by Amber Caravéo
Copyright © Random House Children's Books, 2010

The Random House Group Limited supports the Forest Stewardship Council
(FSC), the leading international forest certification organization. All our titles
that are printed on Greenpeace-approved FSC-certified paper carry the FSC
logo. Our paper procurement policy can be found at
www.rbooks.co.uk/environment

Set in Bembo Schoolbook

Red Fox Books are published by Random House Children's Books,
61–63 Uxbridge Road, London W5 5SA

www.**kids**at**randomhouse**.co.uk
www.**rbooks**.co.uk

Addresses can be

TH

A CIP ibrary.

Printed .0 4TD

For Theo Robinson, one of the very first Gargoylz fans
- **Burchett & Vogler**

For Jake, a little monkey of the first order
- **Leighton Noyes**

Hello, I'm the Web Gargoyle.
Look out for me – I'll be hiding in one
of the pictures in the book.
When you spot me, be sure to make a
note of the secret codeword I'm holding.
The codeword unlocks a secret level
of the amazing Gargoylz game
on our fabulous website at
www.gargoylz.co.uk

Oldacre Primary School

garden

staff car park

staffroom

playing field

playground

hedgehog

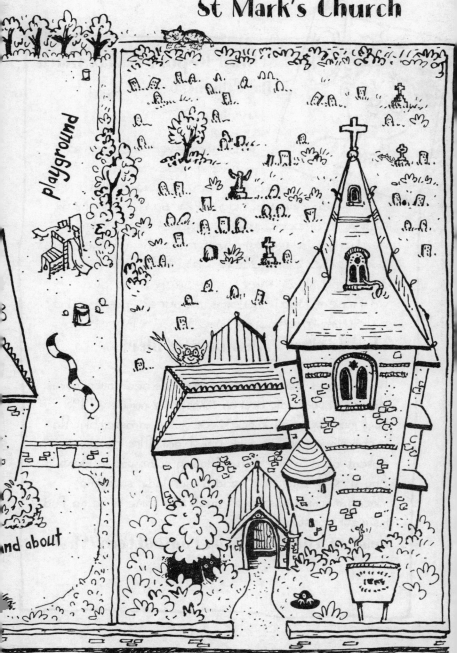

St Mark's Church

playground

and about

School Report - Max Black

Days absent: 0

Days late: 0

Max is never afraid to make a contribution to history lessons. His demonstration of a battering ram using a broom and a bucket was very realistic, although the resulting hole in the classroom door was not ideal.

I worry that Max only seems to play with Ben Neal, but he assures me he has a lot of friends at the local church.

Class teacher - Miss Deirdre Bleet

Max Black's behaviour this term has been outrageous. He has repeatedly broken school rule number 739: boys must not tell 'knock knock' jokes in assembly. He is still playing pranks with Ben Neal. Mrs Pumpkin is absent again after the exploding paint pot incident. And Mrs Simmer, the head dinner lady, says the mincing machine has never been the same since he fed his maths test into it.

Head teacher - Hagatha Hogsbottom (Mrs)

School Report - Ben Neal

Days absent: 0

Days late: 0

This term Ben has
been very inventive in PE.
However, attempting to tightrope-walk
across the hall was a little dangerous
- and used up all the skipping ropes.
He spends far too much time in class
looking out of the window and waving at
the gravestones in the churchyard. He
would be better learning his spellings - a
word he insists on writing as 'spellingz'.

Class teacher - Miss Deirdre Bleet

Ben Neal is always polite, but I am deeply concerned
about his rucksack. It often looks very full - and
not with school books, I am certain. It has sometimes
been seen to wriggle and squirm. I suspect that he
is keeping a pet in there. If so, it is outrageous and
there will be trouble.

Head teacher - Hagatha Hogsbottom (Mrs)

Contents

1. Skeleton Scare   1

2. Candyfloss Suprise   31

3. Picture Perfect   53

4. Fright Night   82

1. Skeleton Scare

"It's Friday evening and it's time for the fair!" exclaimed Max Black, jumping into his imaginary spy rocket and zooming out of Ben's front door. "Let's get there, Agent Neal."

All week Max and his best friend, Ben Neal, had watched the travelling fair being set up on Oldacre village green. Tonight was the opening night!

"Not so fast, Agent Black," said Ben. "We have to wait for my sister and her stupid friend. They're still upstairs doing their hair."

"Arabella and Charlotte should be like

1

me," said Max. He ran his hands through his spiky brown hair. "See? Ready!"

"If only Mum hadn't said we've all got to go together," moaned Ben. "Yuck! Hope no one sees us walking along with *girls*."

At that moment the boys heard an ear-splitting "*Tee-hee-hee-hee-hee!*" Max's spy radar burst into life. Pink frills, goofy teeth, a laugh that could pierce eardrums.

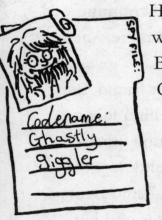

He knew what that meant. It was Enemy Agent Charlotte Boggs, codename: Ghastly Giggler.

"Her giggling's louder than a fire alarm!" complained Ben. "Everyone will look at us."

"Don't worry, Agent Neal," Max whispered as they trailed along the road behind Mrs Neal and the girls. "Super spies like us will soon

2

shake them off at the fair."

At last they arrived at the ticket booth.

"Awesome!"
exclaimed Ben,
gazing at the bright
flashing lights of the
fairground rides.

"Candyfloss!"
sighed Max as the
sweet sugary smell
wafted around them.
"Scrumptious!"

Mrs Neal paid the entrance money and
their hands were stamped with a red big
wheel.

"Now we can go on any ride," said
Ben. "And there's hardly anyone here yet
so there won't be queues."

"We'll start with the carousel," said
Arabella bossily. She pointed a determined
finger at the shiny horses going slowly up
and down.

"*Tee-hee-hee-hee-hee*," giggled Charlotte. "That'll be fun!"

"How boring!" groaned Max.

"And girly!" added Ben.

"Let's find the ghost train!" suggested Max. "I want to go on something spooky."

Ben nodded. "Cool choice!"

"We'll start with the carousel," said Mrs Neal. "After all, Arabella asked first. You can choose next, boys."

Arabella smirked and Charlotte giggled again. Ben looked at Max in horror. They were going to have to stay with the girls for the whole fair — and put up with the Ghastly Giggler!

"Agreed," said Max, to Ben's amazement. "As long as you two don't mind me being sick all over you.

Roundabouts make me ill."

Charlotte stopped mid-giggle.

Arabella's eyes widened with disgust.

"Very well," said Mrs Neal quickly. "Girls, you go on the carousel and boys, you can go on the ghost train." Max and Ben high-fived. "But no mischief," she warned. "I'll be keeping an eye on you."

"Good thinking, Agent Black," commented Ben as he and Max charged off through the crowds.

"We won't have any more trouble with them, Agent Neal," answered Max. "Prepare for a super-scare!"

They zoomed past the dodgems, skirted the hoopla stall and stopped in front of the ghost train.

"Is that it?" said Max in disgust.

Its walls were covered in peeling brown paint and floppy cobwebs. A plastic spider with six legs dangled miserably over the entrance. The sign above said: **THE SCARE OF YOUR LIFE.**

A high-pitched wailing sound was coming from inside.

"How feeble!" exclaimed Max. "It sounds like a mouse with toothache!"

As he spoke, a door at the side opened and a man stepped out wearing a tatty white sheet with two eyeholes.

"If that's a ghost, I'm a pumpkin," said Ben.

"We mustn't give up," said Max. "I expect the fairground people are just making us think it's not scary so we get the fright of our lives when we go in."

Ben cheered up immediately. "You could be right. And it looks old enough to have *real* ghosts in it!" he said. "Let's check it out."

The boys scampered up to the booth, showed their stamped hands and jumped into the front car. The others were empty.

The swing doors flapped open and the car rumbled slowly along a dark tunnel. A weedy scream crackled from a speaker overhead and a ghost on a stick popped up beside them. Round the first corner a coffin lid wobbled open and a vampire with a missing fang sat up and waved. They could see its strings.

"Boring!" scoffed Max.

The car lurched along unsteadily.

Then everything went pitch black and a deep, hollow laugh echoed through the dark. A spotlight flashed on, and a huge, gleaming white skeleton suddenly appeared in front of them.

"At last!" cried Max, delighted. "Things are getting spooky!"

But Ben was gripping the safety bar, his eyes like saucers.

"What's up?" asked Max as the skeleton walked slowly towards them. "You're not scared, are you?"

Ben gulped. "If that's part of the ride, then how come it's standing *on the tracks?*"

Max froze. Ben was right. The skeleton was right in front of them – its ghastly grinning face and long jangling bones lit eerily by the spotlight. And it wasn't being worked by strings or sticks! It turned its empty eye sockets on the boys, staring long and hard. Then it shook its bony fingers up and down as if ready to make a grab for them. The boys yelped in terror. Next there was a dazzling flash of light and the skeleton stepped to the side of the tracks.

"It's alive!" croaked Ben.

"Hello, Max and Ben," the skeleton said in a deep, echoing voice.

Max and Ben leaned as far away from the skeleton as possible while the car chugged slowly past. But they didn't dare take their eyes off it until they had gone round a corner and out of sight.

"Did you see that?" whispered Max.

"It – it knew our names!" stuttered Ben. "It might come after us!"

Suddenly something dropped heavily onto Max's shoulder.

"*Aargghhhh!*" he shrieked, and tried to leap out of the car. "It's got me!"

"Help!" wailed Ben. "We're being attacked!"

"Greetingz!" came a growly purr.

The boys looked up to see Toby, their gargoyle friend, his eyes shining with mischief!

He hopped down
onto Max's lap.
"How did
you get here?"
gasped Ben.
"You gave us
such a fright!"
said Max.

"We saw the
fair being set up
from the church spire," said Toby, flapping
his wings and screwing up his monkey
face excitedly. "It looked like fun so most
of the gargoylz have come along."

The gargoylz were little carved stone
creatures who lived on the church next
door to the boys' school. Max and Ben
were the only humans who knew that
they were alive and that they all had
special powers — which were great for
playing tricks on people.

"We didn't want to miss the fun," called

an eager voice, and Azzan jumped into the front of the car. Theo landed beside him, waving his stripy tail in delight.

"I wouldn't stay here," Max warned them. He glanced around nervously. "There's a really spooky skeleton somewhere . . ."

The gargoylz burst out laughing.

Azzan chuckled so much he snorted fire from his dragony nose.

"That's Rufus," explained Toby. "He's our friend."

"Your friend?" echoed Max, horrified.

"We heard you say the ghost train

wasn't scary enough so we asked him to help out," said Theo. He gave a happy *miaow*. "And it worked!"

"Y-y-you've got a friend who's a skeleton?" gasped Ben.

"He's a gargoyle . . ." began Theo.

". . . whose special power is *turning into a skeleton*," finished Azzan.

The boys grinned with relief.

"Cool power!" exclaimed Max. "It must be great for playing tricks."

"He was really scary!" added Ben. "I can't wait to meet him!"

"He'll want to say hello to you too," said Toby.

"We told him you're our friendz," said Azzan, "so it's OK for you to talk to him . . ."

". . . even though you're humanz," added Theo.

The train passed
a floppy witch
puppet with broken
strings and rattled
on towards some
double doors. The
boys could see
daylight beyond.
The ride was
nearly over.

The gargoylz
jumped out and scampered off.

"Meet us round the back," Toby called
over his shoulder.

When the train ground to a halt,
Max and Ben jumped out and ran round
behind the ride. Toby, Azzan and Theo
were waiting for them.

"Introducing Rufus!" announced Theo.

Something moved the rotten planks at
the back of the ride, and a very strange
gargoyle scrambled out.

Rufus was taller than the other gargoylz, with a huge warty nose and big bulging cheeks. He had wide, hunched shoulders and his muscly arms dangled down to the ground.

"Er, hello," said Ben and Max nervously.

Rufus's face split into an enormous friendly grin. "Hello!" he boomed, waving a pudgy hand. "Did you like my trick?"

"It was awesome," said Max.

"It's not easy," Rufus told them. "But it's very useful for scaring off pesky humanz. Not you two, of course!" he added, giving Max a friendly punch on the arm that nearly knocked him over.

"Show them how you change into a skeleton," said Theo. "Of course, it's not as terrifying as when I turn into a ferocious tiger," he added, "but it's still amazing."

Theo *thought* he became a fierce tiger when he used his special power to change shape, but as he was a very young gargoyle — only 412 years old — he only ever managed a sweet tabby kitten.

"Stand back for a *spook*tacular performance," said Rufus, flexing his massive muscles. He sucked himself in like a balloon deflating. Then, before their amazed eyes, he grew tall and thin and his stone melted away. Now a giant grinning skeleton loomed over the boys, rattling its bones and gnashing its teeth.

Max and Ben clapped wildly as Rufus shrank back into a

gargoyle again and took a bow.

"Got to be off now," Toby said, rubbing his paws together. "We've got lots of rides to try."

The gargoylz scampered away excitedly.

"That sounds like a good idea!" exclaimed Max. "Let's go and try a few more rides too, Agent Neal."

They shot off towards the dodgems and ran straight into Arabella and Charlotte.

"Hello," said Arabella with a beaming smile. She was holding something behind her back.

"Glad we've found you. *Tee-hee-hee-hee-hee!*" Charlotte's giggle was even louder than usual.

"They're up to something," hissed Ben suspiciously.

"Who was scared of a silly little ghost train then?" said Arabella sweetly.

"Poor babies!" snorted Charlotte.

The boys' jaws dropped in amazement.

"How did they know?" Max muttered in Ben's ear.

Arabella pulled a piece of shiny paper out from behind her back and dangled it in front of them. Max and Ben gawped at it. It was a picture of the two boys in the ghost train – their mouths open in utter terror.

"That's us," gasped Ben.

"That flash of light must have been a ride photo," croaked Max. He leaped forward to snatch the embarrassing picture.

But Ben's sister was too quick for him. She whipped it away and skipped off into the busy face-painting tent. Charlotte poked her tongue out and followed, giggling all the way.

"We can't get it back from her in there," moaned Ben. "Someone might see it."

"It's so unfair, Agent Neal," said Max as they mooched away. "The photo doesn't show Rufus's super-spooky skeleton. Anyone would have been scared of that."

"That's true," said Ben, scowling. "But girls don't care about things like that. They're totally unreasonable! What we need, Agent Black, is Secret Plan: Get Our Own Back."

"That's going to take some thinking," said Max. He pointed at the spinning teacups ride. "And there's the place to do it. Spinning always helps my brain work."

The boys raced over and clambered into a teacup. As the ride picked up speed

and the cups began to spin, the boys heard
growly laughter above the music. A spotty
cup flashed by and they caught a glimpse
of three merry stone-coloured creatures
rolling around inside.

"More gargoylz!" shouted Ben in
delight. "There's Zack and Cyrus . . . and
Eli too! I can see the snakes on his head –
they're all tangled together."

"Seeing Cyrus has given me an idea for our secret plan," said Max mysteriously.

As soon as the ride finished, the boys followed their three stony friends to the back of the shooting range.

"We need your help to play a trick on Ben's sister and her awful friend," said Max.

"Yippee!" shouted the gargoylz. "We love tricks."

Max told them about the photo. "So you see how mean the girls are," he explained.

"We want to get our own back on them," added Ben.

Cyrus flexed his long, sharp claws and put on his fiercest face. "I'll frighten them," he growled menacingly.

"Scare the
girlz! Scare the
girlz!" chanted
Zack, shaking
his mane
excitedly,
while Eli's snakes
wriggled in delight.

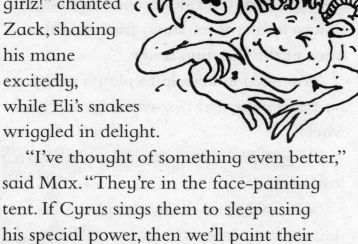

"I've thought of something even better,"
said Max. "They're in the face-painting
tent. If Cyrus sings them to sleep using
his special power, then we'll paint their
faces ourselves and make them look really
ugly!"

"Well," added Ben, "more ugly than
usual, anyway."

"Cyrus, you turn to stone and I'll carry
you in there," said Max. "Everyone will
think you're a prize I won from a stall."

"We'll help with the painting," said Eli.
"I'll turn into a grasss snake and ssslither
in. Then I won't be seen."

"I'll vanish from sight!" yelled Zack, disappearing with an excited **pop!**

Cyrus froze into stone. Max picked him up and marched into the tent. Ben followed behind.

Arabella and Charlotte were having beautiful butterfly wings painted on their cheeks.

"What have you got there?" demanded Arabella, glaring at Cyrus. "It's very ugly."

"*Tee-hee-hee-hee-hee!*" Charlotte tittered.

Max felt Cyrus twitch crossly. "I won it," he said, dumping the frowning gargoyle on Arabella's lap. "If you press its tummy, it sings."

Arabella prodded Cyrus hard.

Ben and Max quickly put their fingers in their ears. They knew Cyrus's power worked on anybody who heard him sing.

Cyrus flung out his arms, opened his mouth and sang a beautiful lullaby at the top of his voice. Snores soon echoed round the tent as, one by one, everyone fell asleep. Zack appeared with a **pop!** and Eli turned from grass snake to gargoyle. Then they all dived headfirst into the box of face paints.

"We'd better hurry before they wake up," said Max.

"Take your time," growled Cyrus. "My song's so powerful they'll stay asleep all night."

"He'sss just boasting as usual," Eli reminded them. "It'll be ten minutesss at the mossst."

Ben put black circles round his sister's eyes and painted a big jagged scar across her cheek.

Max covered Charlotte's face in green paint. Then he drew long white fangs down from her mouth.

The gargoylz blobbed coloured splodges all over the girls' noses.

"Spluttering gutterz!" said Cyrus. "We've done a good job."

"They look like something out of a horror movie," agreed Ben in delight. "Now it's their turn to be embarrassed. I wish we had a camera."

"Gruesome girlz! Gruesome girlz!" declared Zack enthusiastically.

The snakes on Eli's head hissed with laughter.

"Let's see if we can find that photo of us on the ghost train before they wake up," suggested Max.

Ben started to search Arabella's pockets. "There's no sign of it . . ." he said.

Arabella yawned and stretched.

"They're waking up," warned Max. "Hide!"

Max, Ben and the gargoylz ducked down behind a chair.

Arabella opened her eyes and looked around sleepily. Then she caught sight of herself in the mirror. "*Aaaarggghhhh!*" she screamed.

Charlotte woke with a start and stared at her friend in horror. "Your face!" she squawked.

Arabella gawped at her. "And yours!"

They both looked in the mirror together.

"*Aaaargggggghhhhhh!*" they screeched.

Max and Ben and the gargoylz crawled out under the tent wall and collapsed in a heap, rocking with laughter.

"Thanks, gargoylz," said Ben. "We couldn't have done it without you."

"I haven't had so much fun since Zack painted spotsss on the vicar and he thought he had the measlez!" chuckled Eli.

"More ridez! More ridez!" shouted Zack, and the three gargoylz charged off together.

"Well, we may not have found the photo," said Max, "but we've definitely got our own back on the girls. They look hideous!"

"Yup," Ben agreed, grinning happily. "Those girls are so scary the ghost train could do with them!"

2. Candyfloss Surprise

The fair was in full swing when the boys left the face-painting tent.

"I think we'd better steer clear of Arabella and Charlotte for the rest of the evening," said Max. "Just in case they realize it was us who made them into monsters."

"Agreed," said Ben. "What ride shall we go on next?"

"Pieces of eight! Hoist the Jolly Roger!"

The boys spun round. A huge pirate ship was rocking backwards and forwards, getting higher and higher. Something stony-looking was perched on top of the mast.

Max put his spy radar on full power: hooked beak, small piercing eyes, feathery head. He knew what that meant. It was Ira, their gargoyle friend. Ira looked like an eagle that had got mixed up with a parrot, and he behaved like the fiercest pirate on the seven seas.

"Keep the noise down, you scurvy shipmates," Ira squawked at the passengers, who were screaming in delight as the ride got faster.

"That's a funny-looking parrot!" said a woman standing nearby.

"It's almost real," said her friend. "How do they make it speak?"

"Everyone thinks he's part of the ride!" whispered Ben in delight.

When the ship stopped swinging, the
boys were the first to climb aboard. They
waved up at Ira before anyone else got on.

"Warn us if you see my mum coming,"
Ben called up quickly. "Or my sister and
her cackling friend. You can't miss them —
they look like monsters."

"I'll keep a weather eye
out!" agreed Ira, lifting
one wing to shade his
eyes as he peered over
the fairground.

"This is great!"
whooped Ben when the
wooden ship began to move.

"Awesome!" Max laughed. "And we're
safe from enemy agents while Ira's on the
lookout."

"There she blows!" squawked Ira,
pointing a wing into the distance.

Some of the riders giggled at the
strange talking parrot.

Max and Ben scanned the ground
with their superspy watching devices —
codename: eyes. Mrs Neal was marching
through the crowd — and she looked very
cross. Arabella and Charlotte were close
on her heels.

"Your mum must have guessed we did
the girls' makeover,"
groaned Max.

The boys slid down in
their seats, trying not to
be seen.

"Maybe they'll have
gone by the time we get
off," said Ben hopefully.

But as soon as they stood up to get out
of the ship they heard a loud, bossy voice
saying, "Where do you think they are?"

"It's Arabella!" cried Ben. "Look out,
they're coming this way."

"Escape!" yelled Max, grabbing
his arm.

The boys jumped out, dashed through the crowd and bolted into the helter-skelter, where they were hidden from sight. They climbed the stairs to the top, from where they could see Ben's mum and the grisly girls peering into the ghost train.

"We'll slide down and sneak off before they get here," said Ben.

"Wouldn't go down that thing if I were you," said a grumpy voice.

Max stared down into the pile of sacks by the top of the slide. A tubby little gargoyle wearing a gladiator skirt was peeping out at them.

"Hello, Bart!" Max grinned. "Are you enjoying the fair?"

"I was," said Bart miserably, "until I came up here."

"What's wrong?" asked Ben.

"I'm too scared to go down," whispered Bart. "It's ever so high."

"But you climb all over the church," said Max, trying not to laugh. "That's much higher."

"But this is twisty," explained Bart. "I don't like twisty."

"You can't stay here," said Ben. "You might be seen." Far below he could see Arabella looking suspiciously at the door of the helter-skelter. "And we've got to get away quickly."

"Come down with me," suggested Max.

"OK," said Bart doubtfully. "But I won't like it."

"I'll go first." Ben grabbed a sack and shot out of sight. Max got into his and Bart hid inside it.

"Ready?" asked Max.

There was a grunt from the sack.
Max pushed off.

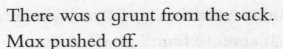

"**Arghhhhh!**"
yelled Bart, as they
shot off down the slide.

"**wheeee!**"
cried Max as they
rocketed round
the bends.

"**Oomph!**"
they both breathed as
they skidded into Ben
on the landing pad at
the bottom.

"You can come out now, Bart," said Max, poking his head into the sack. "There's no one around. Hope you weren't too scared."

Bart hopped out of the sack and headed straight back up the helter–skelter steps.

"Scared?" he exclaimed indignantly. "Dangling drainpipes, that was more fun than when we polished the bottom of the vicar's shoes and he skidded up the aisle! I'm having another go!"

The boys burst out laughing.

"I'll come with you," said Ben eagerly, but Max's spy radar had burst into action: pigtails bobbing, fists clenched, face like a monster. It was Enemy Agent Arabella Neal, codename: Manic Monitor – and the Ghastly Giggler was right behind her.

"We've got to go," Max hissed urgently. "The girls are coming."

They sped off past the hoopla and the coconut shy.

"Quick!" panted Ben. "Behind the Wild West lasso stall."

They threw themselves down behind one of the large plastic cactuses. People were taking turns to throw a loop of rope over the spiky tops.

"We should be safe here," whispered Max, looking around cautiously.

Opposite them was a stall with bulging bags labelled CANDYFLOSS hanging all around it. A woman was standing over a rotating drum, spinning the sugary fluff onto sticks.

"Look at that." Max nudged Ben. "It smells scrumptious. When the coast's clear, let's go and buy some."

"Good plan, Agent Black!" said Ben. "Although that bag's a bit weird."

The nearest bag was swinging all by itself. And something stone-coloured was moving about inside it.

"I can see a dragony tail!" cried Ben.

"And a long pointy snout," added Max.

The boys edged closer for a better look.

"It's Barney!" gasped Max. "What's he doing in there?"

"He's eating the candyfloss!" said Ben. "Come on. We'd better buy him before someone sees him!"

"Good thinking," said Max, looking

around. "There are no enemy agents in sight."

They dashed for the stall. But as they got there, the stallholder was just handing the bag with Barney inside it to a little girl as her mother handed over the money.

Barney was desperately trying to hide himself, but he'd eaten too much of the candyfloss. His unhappy face was pressed up against the inside of the plastic bag.

"We've got to rescue him," said Max urgently. "Let's follow them."

As they crept along behind the little girl and her mother, the boys could hear the girl complaining in a loud voice. "It's too heavy!" she moaned.

"Nonsense," said her mother. "Candyfloss is very light."

"This isn't," said the girl. "And I wanted pink – not white!"

"They only had white," said her mother.

Ben stopped suddenly. "I've got a brilliant idea," he whispered to Max.

"It had better be quick," said Max urgently. "As soon as she opens the bag she'll see Barney."

"All we have to do is find another stall and buy a bag of pink candyfloss," said Ben with a grin. "Then we swap with the little girl and Barney's saved."

"Awesome, Agent Neal!" exclaimed Max. "Look, she's having a go on the hook-a-penguin. She'll be busy for a few minutes. Let's split up and search. That way we've got more chance of finding pink candyfloss somewhere."

"Synchronize watches," said Ben. "See

you back here in five minutes. And avoid all enemy agents!"

Three and a half minutes later, Max and Ben rushed up to each other at the hook-a-penguin stall. They were both carrying two bags of pink candyfloss.

"Success!" panted Ben. "I got an extra one for us."

"Good thinking, Agent Neal," said Max. "So did I!"

The little girl had just managed to hook a penguin.

"Hurry!" gasped Max. "She's opening the bag!"

"Turbo speed, Agent Black!" cried Ben.

They skidded to a halt in front of the girl and her mother.

"Excuse me," began Max in his politest voice. "We . . . um . . . got this for you." He held out one of his bags of fluffy candyfloss.

"We heard you wanted pink not white," explained Ben. "Would you like to swap? We like white best, you see."

"How kind," said the mother in surprise.

Max and the little girl swapped candyfloss bags.

"Thank you," said the little girl, gazing happily at the pink candyfloss.

The boys scampered off. When they were safely behind the waltzer, Max let a very sticky Barney out of the bag.

"You saved me!" he cried. "I thought I was going to be eaten." He shuddered. "Or even worse – that the little human might see that I'm alive. I tried making one of my smellz to frighten her off but it stayed in the bag and nearly choked me!"

Barney's special power was doing bottom burps that were so pongy they could clear a room.

"What were you doing in there?" asked Max, helping the little gargoyle to peel the sticky candyfloss off his tail and ears.

"I didn't mean to be in the bag," said Barney, licking his paws. "I jumped into the drum to eat some of this wonderful sticky stuff but somehow I got bagged and

tagged, and next thing I knew I
was hanging up at the front of the stall!"
He looked around. "Must go and tell
the others I nearly got eaten." He
scampered off.

"We deserve an exciting
ride after that," said Max.

"And there it is," Ben
replied, pointing at the
chairplanes, which
were coming to a stop.
They ran over and
scrambled into one
of the silver planes. It
swung gently as they
settled themselves in.

"We were just in time," said Ben,
looking out across the fair. "Mum's
coming this way and she looks furious."

"At least she hasn't spotted us yet," said
Max. He opened one of the bags. "Have
some candyfloss."

Ben took a handful. "Yummm . . . this is good."

"Stickily scrumptious!" agreed Max.

They'd just munched their way through a whole bag when the chairplanes began to move, slowly at first and then faster and faster.

"Awesome!" yelled Max as their plane sped round at a steep angle. "It's making my tummy tingle!"

They were whizzing so quickly now, the ground was just a blur.

"I'm beginning to feel sick," groaned Ben, clutching the rail.

"My tummy's turning somersaults," said Max. "I hope my dinner doesn't come back up."

At last the ride slowed to a halt.

"Oh no!" said Ben. "Mum's down by the exit. We can't escape this time." He clutched the bags of candyfloss and he and Max climbed out of their plane.

"I've just had a brilliant idea to get us out of trouble," Max whispered as they walked down the steps. "We give our last two bags of candyfloss to the girls."

"Are you sure?" said Ben doubtfully. "We might want them later. I'm feeling better already."

"We have no choice," said Max. "It's a hard life being a superspy."

They walked slowly over to Ben's mum and the two girls. Arabella and Charlotte glowered at them, their painted faces screwed up in big ugly frowns. Mrs Neal wagged an angry finger, but before she could say anything, Max jumped in.

"We shouldn't have made you look horrible," he said quickly to the girls. "We've bought you some candyfloss to

say sorry." Ben thrust the two bags at
Arabella and Charlotte.

"Er . . . thank you," said the girls,
looking astonished as they grabbed the
candyfloss and began to munch.

"It was a silly thing to do," said Ben's
mum. "But I'm glad you're all friends
again. Now let's all go on a ride together."

The girls tried to speak but their
mouths were still full of candyfloss.

Max saw his chance. "Dodgems?" he
suggested quickly.

The boys didn't wait to hear the answer. They darted off towards the bright flashing lights of the electric cars.

"Brilliant, Agent Black," said Ben as they jumped into their seats. "We got ourselves out of trouble and we made the girls look sillier than a troll in a tutu."

Max grinned. "And we're on a cool ride!" He looked over at Arabella and Charlotte, who were driving around slowly. "Let's give those monsters a bump!"

3. Picture Perfect

Max skidded up to Ben's house, trainers
smoking. Before he had a chance to
knock at the door, Ben flung it open and
hurried him up to his bedroom.

"I've called you over for an emergency
Saturday morning spy meeting," he said, a
worried frown on his face.

"That sounds serious, Agent Neal," said
Max. "What's happened?"

"It's that ghost train photo," Ben told
him.

"The one where we look terrified?"
asked Max.

Ben nodded solemnly. "My sister says

she's going to put it up on the school notice board."

Max gawped in horror. "But everyone went to the fair! They'll all know that that ride wasn't scary. We'll never be able to show our faces at school ever again!"

"We'll have to go into hiding," agreed Ben, "change our names – leave the country—"

"I don't understand," Max burst in. "We said sorry for painting ugly faces on Arabella and Charlotte. *And* we gave them candyfloss. What more does she want?"

"She's cross with me," Ben told him. "I put her favourite doll in her lunchbox and sailed it on the garden pond to see if it would float."

"Good experiment," said Max. "Did it work?"

"It capsized," admitted Ben dolefully. "She found the lunchbox full of goldfish and a frog eating her doll's party dress. She went mad."

"Girls!" sighed Max. "They get upset over the silliest things. Cheer up, Agent Neal, we have a Secret Mission: Find Photo."

"Brilliant, Agent Black!" Ben cheered up immediately. "My horrible sister's downstairs trying to wash the weed out of her doll's hair. We'll sneak into her room and look for the photo. Shouldn't be a problem for super spies like us."

Silently, they crept into Arabella's
bedroom.

"Yuck!" whispered Max as he stumbled
over the fluffy unicorn rug. "It's all pink
and girly in here. And there's no sign of
the photo."

"I bet she's hidden it somewhere," said
Ben. He opened a big sparkly box marked
TOP SECRET and began to rummage
through the contents.

Suddenly, the
door flew open
and Arabella stood
there, her face
like thunder. Ben
jumped, spilling the
contents of the box
all over the floor.

"Mum!"
shrieked Arabella.

Mrs Neal appeared and frowned at the
mess.

"We were just . . . tidying," stammered
Max.

"It's our good deed for the day," added
Ben, trying to look innocent.

"It looks more like when you played
shipwrecks in here last week!" Mrs Neal
told him crossly. "It took days to dry
Arabella's mattress out."

"Can we go to the shops, Mum?" asked
Arabella. "I have some" – she fixed the

boys with an evil smile – "*photocopying* for *school* to do."

Max and Ben looked at each other in horror. They knew what that meant.

Arabella was going to make copies of the photo. Then she'd be able to put them all over the school.

"Yes, of course," said Mrs Neal as she left the room. Max gulped and Ben looked panic-stricken. "But I've got a few jobs to finish first. Come on, boys. Out!"

Max and Ben fled to the garden.

"We've got to find that photo before it's turned into a thousand copies," groaned Ben. "But we can't risk being caught in Arabella's room again."

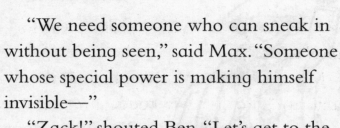

"We need someone who can sneak in without being seen," said Max. "Someone whose special power is making himself invisible—"

"Zack!" shouted Ben. "Let's get to the church and find that gargoyle. I'll take my rucksack to bring him back in."

Two minutes later the boys were zooming at top speed towards the church in their imaginary monster spy truck.

"Coo—eee!" came a merry voice along the road.

Ben's next-door neighbour, old Mrs Tabkin, was coming towards them. "You boys are always in a rush," she chuckled, planting herself in the middle of the pavement.

"We're going to the church . . ." panted Ben.

". . . to meet some . . . friends," added Max, trying to edge round her.

"How lucky!" exclaimed Mrs Tabkin. "I've got a note for the vicar. You can deliver it."

She plunged her hand into her large bag and rummaged around. The boys looked at each other in dismay.

"It's in here somewhere," Mrs Tabkin
muttered, pulling out scarves and cough
drops for the boys to hold. "Oh! I
remember now," she said at last as she
stuffed everything back in. "I posted it this
morning!"

Hastily shouting goodbye, Max and
Ben raced off round the corner – and
collided with Max's mum, knocking her
bags of shopping to the ground.

Max rescued a bunch of bananas from
a hedge. "Sorry!" he gasped.

"We're in a hurry, you see," Ben explained as he chased a potato along the pavement.

"You should look where you're going!" said Mrs Black crossly. "Now make yourselves useful and help me carry all this home."

Max and Ben trailed along behind her, each carrying a shopping bag. Time was running out. At any minute Arabella could be setting off for the printing shop.

"I thought we'd never get here!" said Ben

as the boys roared into the churchyard half an hour later.

"There's only one problem," said Max, frowning. "I can't see any gargoylz."

Ben scanned the church roof and gutters. "You're right!" he exclaimed. He looked among the gravestones. "Not a scale or a tail! How are we going to get the photo back now?"

Max sniffed the air. "Someone's baking!" he gasped. "Awesome!"

"It smells good," agreed Ben. "But we've got to concentrate on finding the gargoylz."

"I know where they'll be," said Max mysteriously. "Follow me, Agent Neal."

He led the way towards the smell.
Next door to the church was the vicar's
house. They peered over the wall. A freshly
baked cake was steaming by an open
window. And crouched underneath was
a crowd of gargoylz – chomping noisily
on a pile of chocolate chip muffins.

"Good detective work, Agent Black!"
said Ben with a grin. "Gargoylz love
cakes."

Max gazed longingly at the muffins.
"So do I," he said.

"Greetingz, boyz!" Toby waved a sticky
paw at them.

"The vicar's wife baked these,"
explained Eli as he fed bits of muffin to
the wriggling snakes on his head. "But
she burned them and threw them out."

"They're still delicious though," added
Cyrus, sinking his fangs into the biggest

muffin he could find.

"Better than ship's biscuits!" squawked Ira.

"Barney rescued them for us," said Toby. "There's plenty to share."

Scooping up the cakes, the gargoylz scampered over the wall to join the boys. They all tucked in and the pile of muffins was soon gone.

"What a feast," sighed Ben, flopping back on the grass.

"Dangling drainpipes!" exclaimed Cyrus, rubbing his tummy. "I'm stuffed."

Max suddenly leaped to his feet. "The photo!" he yelped. "We've forgotten our secret mission, Agent Neal!"

Ben went pale. "We need Zack – and he's not here!"

"Yes I am!" came a voice from the wall. There was a **pop!** and Zack appeared, shaking crumbs out of his shaggy mane. "Ate nine – no, ten – and a half muffins!"

"So that's why the pile went down so quickly!" said Ben.

"We need your help, Zack," said Max.

He explained about the embarrassing photo and how Arabella had threatened to show it to everyone at school.

"We'd never have let Rufus scare you if we'd known what was going to happen," said Toby solemnly. "You can't trust girlz."

"Now we just *have* to get the photo back," said Ben.

"Zack, could you make yourself invisible and sneak into Arabella's room to find it?" asked Max.

"No problem!" declared Zack, bouncing up and down in delight.

"I'll take you home in my rucksack—" began Ben, but Zack had already vanished with a loud **pop!**

"I know the way!" they heard his cheery voice in the distance. "See you there."

"It's time to get in our secret monster spy truck," said Max. "Bye, gargoylz!"

"I'll come with you," said Toby, "to watch TV . . . I mean, to keep an eye on Zack."

"OK . . ." Ben groaned as Toby hopped into his rucksack. "But I wish you hadn't eaten so many muffins. You're extra heavy!"

Toby chuckled as they zoomed off towards Ben's house.

To their relief Arabella was still at home. She was in the kitchen, pestering her mum to take her to the print shop. The boys burst into Ben's bedroom and found Zack running up and down the bookshelves, popping in and out of sight with excitement.

"Window was open," he explained. "Climbed up the drainpipe."

Toby turned on the television. An old spy film was on. He sighed happily and lay back on Ben's pillow to watch it.

"I thought you were here to keep an eye on Zack!" said Max with a grin.

"I am," said Toby, eyes glued to the TV.

Ben caught hold of Zack as he flashed by and sat him on his chair. "The photo's somewhere in my sister's room," he told the eager gargoyle, "and she'll be up to get it at any minute, so you have to move fast."

"You can't miss her bedroom," Max told him. "Just follow the yucky flowery smell."

"Back in a jiff!" said Zack, dashing out of the door.

"Don't forget to be invisible!" Max yelled after him.

They heard a faint **pop!** from the landing.

Minutes passed. Max and Ben paced anxiously up and down Ben's room.

"Supposing Zack can't find the photo!" muttered Max.

"What if Arabella's got it on her?" said Ben with a worried frown.

"You're blocking my view of the TV!" complained Toby. "It's getting to the best bit. These two spies have to—"

Just then there was a **pop!** and Zack appeared in the middle of the carpet, a pile of photographs in his paw.

"Great work, Zack!" Ben said,

grabbing them eagerly and spreading them out on the floor. "We've foiled her stupid plan."

Max rifled through the scattered photos and frowned. "But these are all of Arabella when she was a toddler," he said.

"Ours must be here somewhere!" insisted Ben. He crawled around, frantically throwing photos aside. "Arabella having a tantrum . . . Arabella with a bucket on her head . . . Arabella stuffing a banana in her mouth."

"I wonder why she's kept these," said Max. "She'd be so upset if anyone saw them. She looks really stupid."

"This is the best one . . ." Ben couldn't help laughing. "Arabella covered in cow poo!"

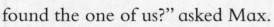

"But have you found the one of us?" asked Max.

"There's no sign of it," said Ben in despair.

They heard footsteps on the stairs and then Arabella's bedroom door banged shut. The boys looked horrified. She must have gone to get the dreaded picture.

"What are we going to do, Agent Neal?" asked Max desperately.

Toby suddenly piped up from the bed. "In this film there are two spies and they have to—"

"We haven't got time to hear about

spy films," said Ben desperately. "This is
serious."

"That's why I'm telling you," said Toby.
"The film's given me an idea."

"Is it a prank? Is it a prank?" asked
Zack eagerly.

Toby waddled to the edge of the bed.
"Not exactly, but it will get the photo
back."

"Ready in five minutes, Arabella?" they heard Ben's mum calling.

"What's the plan, Toby?" said Max urgently.

"You do an exchange," said Toby solemnly.

"An exchange?" Ben frowned. "What do you mean?"

"The spies in the film both had something the other one wanted," explained Toby. "So they swapped, and everyone was happy!"

"Arabella's bound to want her baby photos back . . ." said Ben thoughtfully, a slow smile spreading across his face.

"It's brilliant!" exclaimed Max. "We tell Arabella we've got these embarrassing pictures of her to show everyone. Then we say we'll give them back if she returns our ghost train photo."

"I'll write her a note," said Ben, scribbling on a piece of paper.

Toby nodded. "Like a real spy."

"How about this?" said Ben a few minutes later, showing them the note.

To Enemy Agent Arabella Neal,
We have got ~~imbarissing emmbarasing~~ silly photos of you. And we're not afraid to use them. If you want them back, meet us at the bottom of the garden in two minutes. Bring the ghost train photo.
From Secret Agent Ben Neal.
P.S. They're worse than the one attached to this letter!

"I'll give her the picture where she's got her head in a bucket," said Ben, "to show we mean business."

He jumped
up, dived into
his wardrobe
and emerged
wearing an
orange wig,
sunglasses and a
big floppy hat.

Max, Toby
and Zack burst out
laughing.

"Spies always wear a disguise,"
explained Ben. He wrapped the note
around the photo of bucket-head Arabella,
tiptoed off to her bedroom door and slid
the note underneath it. When he got back
to his room, everyone was in disguise.
Max had pulled on Ben's dressing gown
back to front, Toby had a sock over his
head and Zack was wearing flippers.

Five seconds later a horrified scream
rang out.

"I think your plan's working, Toby," said Max with glee. "Let's get down the garden to wait for her."

Max, Ben, Toby and Zack hid behind the shed. Soon they saw the back door of the house open and Ben's sister storm out.

"She looks really cross." Toby giggled. "This'll be better than when Cyrus sang the vicar to sleep at a christening and he fell in the font."

Arabella came down to the bottom of the garden and looked around angrily. She was holding the photo. Ben stepped out and snuck up behind her, pulling the brim of his hat down over his face.

"Enemy Agent Arabella Neal?" he hissed in her ear in his best mysterious spy voice.

Arabella jumped with fright. "Of course!" she said irritably.

"Are you ready for the exchange?"

"Just give me my pictures," she snapped, holding out her hand. "*Now!*"

"Not until you hand over the photo of Agent Black and Agent Neal," growled Ben. "And if you don't, we'll show your friends *all* the ones we've got of you. Do you really want them to see you with a face full of banana or sitting in a cowpat?"

Shrieking with fury, Arabella threw the ghost train photograph down on the rockery. Ben placed her photos in a pile next to it, snatched up the one of him and Max and disappeared behind the shed again.

Arabella picked up her pictures and ran back to the house.

"You haven't heard the last of this!" she
yelled.

Ben showed the ghost train photo to his
delighted friends.

"I think we *have* heard the last of it,"
said Max. "That was excellent spy work,
Agent Neal."

"Good swap! Good swap!" chanted
Zack, flapping about in his flippers.

Ben ripped the photo into little pieces
as Max looked on approvingly. "Thanks,
gargoylz," Ben said. "Now no one will
ever know we were scared on the ghost
train!"

4. Fright Night

Max and Ben whizzed into the playground in their superspy rocket-car.

"I can't believe we're early on a Monday morning," said Max.

"Awesome!" exclaimed Ben. "That gives us more gargoyle time!"

They were making for the wall between the churchyard and the school when a scream filled the air.

"It's coming from a Year Six classroom," said Max.

"Let's investigate, Agent Black," suggested Ben. "It sounds interesting."

They dashed inside.

A crowd of children had already gathered in Miss True's classroom. Charlotte Boggs, the Ghastly Giggler, was standing on a chair. She wasn't giggling now. She was whimpering.

Arabella pulled at her skirt. "What's the matter?" she demanded in her loudest monitor's voice.

"It was awful," wailed Charlotte, wringing her hands. "So huge and evil . . . and it looked straight at me. I thought I was done for."

"Tell me what you saw," demanded Arabella.

"A ghost?" said Ben hopefully.

"A monster?" suggested Max.

"A . . . mouse!" gulped Charlotte.

 "You were afraid of a tiny little mouse!" burst out Max.

"It was probably more scared of you,"

Ben told her pityingly.

Charlotte's eyes narrowed. "You can't talk," she said loudly to the boys. "You were terrified on the silly ghost train at the fair."

Everyone in the class turned to stare at Max and Ben. Arabella gave an evil grin.

"The ghost train was rubbish," someone called from the door. "Everyone knows that." Max's spy radar jumped into life: shaved head, big fists, knuckles like rocks. He knew what that meant. It was Enemy Agent Barry Price, also known as The Basher, codename: School Bully.

SPY FILE!

Codename:
School
Bully

Max and Ben groaned. What bad luck that he happened to be passing just at that moment.

The Basher strode up to Max and Ben
and stuck his face into theirs. "I took my
cousin on that stupid ride. She wasn't
scared and she's only four. You two are
weedy wimps!"

Everyone laughed and The Basher gave an evil grin.

Max and Ben knew there was only one thing for it. They stormed off.

At morning break Barry followed the boys around the playground.

"Scaredy-cats," he sneered. "Little babies frightened by silly plastic witches and vampires."

A group of girls stopped their skipping game and tittered.

"Everyone's laughing," groaned Max. "Let's take cover, Agent Neal."

They hid in the toilets until the bell went.

"That was the worst playtime in the history of worst playtimes," complained Ben. "If only we could tell everyone about Rufus and what a scary skeleton he was."

"We need to make a dash for our classroom," said Max, opening the door and peering down the corridor. "No sign of Barry—"

"**Boo!**" The Basher leaped out from behind a pot plant. "Made you jump!" he crowed.

Max and Ben sprinted for the safety of their classroom.

"At least he can't follow us in here," said Ben, slumping onto his chair. Then he groaned. "I've just remembered. Year Four get together after lunch for Story Sharing. We'll have Barry Price for a whole hour and he's sure to keep teasing us. Everyone else will join in. It will be a disaster."

But Max was looking thoughtful.
"Maybe not, Agent Neal," he said. "We
could use the lesson to get our own back
on The Basher. We just need a secret plan."

"Good thinking, Agent Black," said
Ben with a grin. "Let's see if the gargoylz
want to help."

Straight after
lunch they made
for the churchyard
wall. Toby was
crouched over
one of the church
windows.

"Greetingz!" he
called as he flew
down to join them.

"We need help,"
said Ben urgently. "The Basher's making
everyone laugh at us."

"He's telling them we were frightened by that stupid ghost train," explained Max. "And we can't tell them that Rufus was the one who really scared us."

Toby frowned. "I could shoot acornz at him with my catapult or we could get Azzan to burn his bottom," he said. "But I reckon he needs a really good scare."

"That's it!" exclaimed Max. "We'll use Rufus's secret power to frighten The Basher!"

"Rufus would love that," said Toby. "He likes tricks as much as the rest of us gargoylz."

"Awesome!" cried Ben, high-fiving with Max and Toby. "But how are we going to do it?"

"With Secret Plan: Scary Skeleton!" replied Max. "But I haven't quite worked it all out yet."

After lunch, Year Four gathered in the library for Story Sharing. To the boys' horror, Barry Price came and sat next to them.

"I'll protect you from the nasty ghosties," he said, and everyone laughed.

"Quiet please . . ." came a feeble voice.

Max activated his spy radar: short and dumpy, limp brown hair, twitchy nose. He knew what that meant. It was Enemy Agent Miss Bleet, codename: Wimpy Teacher.

"Who's got a story to share with us today?" she asked.

"Better not be scary," Barry called
out. "Or Max and Ben will run away
screaming!"

Max could feel his face going red.
And then it came to him. He remembered
that Barry's house overlooked the
graveyard and suddenly he knew what to
do for their secret plan.

He put his hand up. "I've got a really
cool story," he said. "It's about the church
next door."

Miss Bleet looked doubtful. "I hope
it's good this time," she said. "Not like

last week. 'How I flooded the toilets and pretended to be a killer shark' was not a proper story."

"This one is, honestly!" Max promised, jumping up before Miss Bleet could protest.

"I am going to tell you all a true story," he told his audience in a mysterious voice. "I heard it from my granddad, and he heard it from his granddad, and he heard it from—"

Miss Bleet raised an eyebrow.

"Anyway," said Max, "prepare for the legend of Oldacre Church—"

"There is no legend," interrupted Barry rudely. "I should know. I live next door to the church."

"Yes, there is," Max went on. "The Legend of the Skeleton Dance. You see, hundreds of years ago, Nick Turnip, a wicked highwayman, was buried in the graveyard. No one knows where his grave is, but since then, every fifty years, on his birthday, his skeleton comes out of the ground and dances around the gravestones."

Everyone in Year Four was listening hard now.

"My granddad thought it was a made-up story until one dark and windy night," Max told them.

Ben made whistling noises, pretending to be the wind. Some of the girls shivered.

"He was walking home from the village," continued Max in a hushed tone, "when, just as the clock was striking, he saw strange lights darting amongst the gravestones."

A shudder went through the audience.

"Granddad crept into the churchyard to see what was going on and he couldn't believe his eyes!"

"**OoooOohhhh!**" wailed Ben, making Miss Bleet jump out of her skin.

Max lowered his voice to a hoarse whisper. "Under the full moon, just as the legend had said, a huge skeleton was rattling his bones in a terrifying dance. And spooky lights flickered all around him!"

Poppy and Tiffany clutched each other and Miss Bleet fanned herself with a hanky.

"That was exactly fifty years ago," Max finished triumphantly. "Tonight, under the full moon, the fearsome skeleton of the highwayman will dance again! Oh, and I forgot to say – it'll be at eight o'clock precisely."

He looked around at his audience, which was hanging on his every word – even Barry Price.

Duncan was the first to come out of the spell. He glanced at The Basher's pale face and grinned. "Are you scared, Barry?" he demanded.

"Of course not," blustered Barry. "Max made it up. It's a load of rubbish."

"It's true, honest!" said Max.

Ben nodded. "I've heard of the legend too," he said, opening his blue eyes wide and putting on his most innocent face. It always worked on the dinner ladies, who gave him extra choco-crisp for pudding.

"Why don't you look out tonight, Barry?" Max suggested. "If you're lucky you might see Nick Turnip's bones for yourself."

The Basher's eyes grew wider.

"Dare you to look," said Ben. "Max and I will be there at eight o'clock to see the skeleton ourselves, so we'll know if you do."

"I'll be watching," growled Barry, "and I don't care how many skeletons there are, they don't frighten me!"

"I'm sure you've all got better things to do than wander around the churchyard," said Miss Bleet, mopping her brow with the board rubber. "Now let's have a nice story about kittens . . ."

★ ★ ★

Straight after school, Max and Ben dashed
over to the churchyard and told Toby the
story that Max had made up.

"We need you gargoylz to hold torches
to make the flickering lights," finished Ben.
"And of course Rufus to be our skeleton.
Will you do it?"

"Of course!" Toby chuckled. "We'll be
ready. I'll even get Rufus to practise his
dancing. He hasn't done any for three
hundred yearz." He flew up to the church
roof and out of sight.

"That's the gargoylz sorted," said Max. "Now we need an excuse to come out tonight."

"Ask your mum if I can stay at your house," suggested Ben. "I'll make sure I forget my pyjamas and then we'll have to go back to my house to get them."

"And on the way back, we'll visit the churchyard," said Max happily. "Good thinking, Agent Neal."

Once the sleepover had been arranged with their mums, Max and Ben sat in Max's bedroom, keeping a close eye on the clock.

"It's half past seven," whispered Max. "Time to get going." He grabbed some torches. "The gargoylz will be needing these."

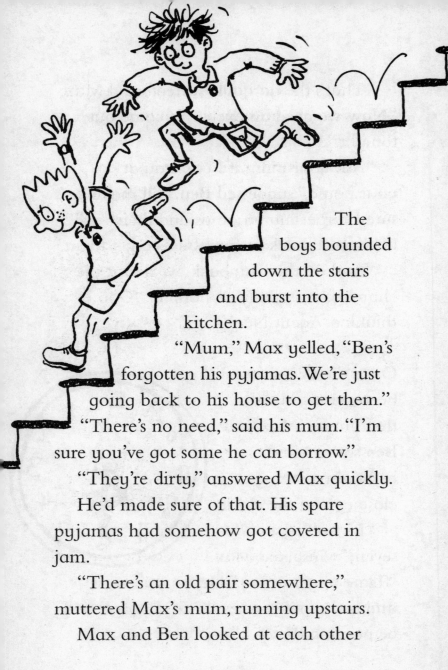

The boys bounded down the stairs and burst into the kitchen.

"Mum," Max yelled, "Ben's forgotten his pyjamas. We're just going back to his house to get them."

"There's no need," said his mum. "I'm sure you've got some he can borrow."

"They're dirty," answered Max quickly. He'd made sure of that. His spare pyjamas had somehow got covered in jam.

"There's an old pair somewhere," muttered Max's mum, running upstairs. Max and Ben looked at each other in horror. If she found Ben some pyjamas, they wouldn't have an excuse to go to the churchyard.

"The Basher will look out and see we're not there," hissed Ben. "He'll think we're too scared to come. We'll never live it down."

"Here we are, Ben." Mrs Black came back into the kitchen holding up a pair of fluffy blue pyjamas covered in teddies.

"I wore those when I was four!" cried Max. "They won't fit Ben."

His mum held them up against Ben, who tried to look as big as possible. "I suppose not," she sighed. "All right, you can go, but be back by half past eight."

The boys sped to Ben's house, squashed together on Max's bike. They grabbed the pyjamas and then headed for the churchyard. By the time they arrived, it was good and dark.

"Greetingz!" came a voice from a deep shadow near the church porch.

Max and Ben ran over. Toby, Rufus, Theo and Ira were squatting there, waiting eagerly.

Pop! Zack appeared next to them. "Spooking time! Spooking time!" he announced.

Max gave the gargoylz their instructions and handed out the torches.

Then the boys and the gargoylz crept round to the back of the church. While the gargoylz hid behind headstones, the boys peered up over the wall and across Barry's garden to his bedroom window, which looked right over the churchyard.

"There's The Basher," said Ben, pointing as a shaved head came into view. Max waved up at Barry, who opened the window and pulled an ugly face.

He smirked at them. "Hello, losers!"

"Ready for Nick Turnip's skeleton?" called Max.

"There's no such thing!" growled Barry.

"Scurvy landlubber," squawked Ira quietly. "Make him walk the plank!"

"No need," muttered Rufus. "He'll soon change his tune when he sees my skeleton."

At that very moment the church clock began to strike eight.

"Go, gargoylz!" whispered Max.

Zack, Theo and Ira ran around between the gravestones, flashing the torches. Toby took to the air, making his light bob and dive all over the place.

"Now that looks really spooky," said Ben, impressed. "Just like in your legend."

"Barry's enjoying it!" Max laughed.

They looked up to see The Basher with his mouth open in utter astonishment.

Toby landed behind a stone angel and shone his torch beam at a large headstone beside him. Right on cue, Rufus rose slowly into view, his huge skeleton glowing eerily in the light. It looked just as if he was floating out of the grave.

"Awesome!" whispered Ben.

Rufus began to dance with slow, jerky movements.

"Super creepy!" said Max. He peered up at Barry's window and nudged Ben. "Plan's working."

The Basher was frozen in terror. His eyes were wide and staring and his mouth was opening and closing like a fish. He pointed a shaky finger at the skeleton.

Rufus danced closer and closer to

Barry's house. Then, amazingly, he began
to rise up in the air until he was level
with Barry's window. Max and Ben could
see Toby holding onto Rufus behind his
back and flapping his wings frantically
with the effort of keeping him in mid-air.

But all The Basher could see was
the bony skeleton with its ghastly grin
getting nearer and nearer. The boys
stifled their giggles.

"*Aaarggghhh!*" Barry screamed.

"Brilliant!" called Max. "Now, everybody hide."

Rufus reached out dramatically with his bony arms just as the other gargoylz switched off the torches, plunging the churchyard into darkness again. Then Rufus shrank back into his stony form and all the gargoylz scuttled out of sight.

A light came on in Barry's bedroom and Max and Ben saw Barry's mum run into the room.

"Dead highwayman skeleton!" they heard him wail, leaping into her arms. "It danced. It came towards me. It was horrible!"

"There, there, my precious," said Mrs Price, stroking Barry's head soothingly. "You must have had a nasty dream."

Max and Ben grinned and high-fived
as the gargoylz bounded over to join
them.

"That secret plan was awesome," said
Max. "Brilliant bones, Rufus."

Rufus flexed
his muscles.
"My most
*spook*tacular
performance
yet," he said,
showing his
fangs in a big
grin.

"Spluttering
skeletonz!" said Toby. "We haven't had
so much fun since we put a kipper in the
vicar's pocket and he was followed by all
the local cats."

"And one thing's for sure," added Ben.
"Barry won't tease us about being scared
ever again!"

"It was the best fright in the history of best frights!" declared Max, and all the gargoylz cheered loudly.

Gargoylz Fact File

Full name: Tobias the Third
Known as: Toby
Special Power: Flying
Likes: All kinds of pranks and mischief – especially playing jokes on the vicar
Dislikes: Mrs Hogsbottom, garden gnomes

Full name: Barnabas
Known as: Barney
Special Power: Making big stinks!
Likes: Cookiez
Dislikes: Being surprised by humanz

Name: Eli
Special Power: Turning into a grass snake
Likes: Sssports Day, Ssslithering
Dislikes: Ssscary ssstories

Full name: Bartholomew

Known as: Bart

Special Power: Burping spiders

Likes: Being grumpy

Dislikes: Being told to cheer up

Full name: Theophilus

Known as: Theo

Special Power: Turning into a ferocious tiger (well, tabby kitten!)

Likes: Sunny spots and cosy places

Dislikes: Rain

Full name: Zackary

Known as: Zack

Special Power: Making himself invisible to humanz

Likes: Bouncing around, eating bramblz, thistlz, and anything with Pricklz!

Dislikes: Keeping still

Name: Azzan

Special Power: Breathing fire

Likes: Surprises

Dislikes: Smoke going up his nose and making him sneeze

Name: Ira

Special Power: Making it rain

Likes: Making humanz walk the plank

Dislikes: Being bored

Name: Cyrus

Special Power: Singing lullabies to send humanz to sleep

Likes: Fun dayz out

Dislikes: Snoring

Name: Rufus

Special Power: Turning into a skeleton

Likes: Playing spooky tricks

Dislikes: Squeezing into small spaces